Dinosaur Goes to Israel

To our whole *mishpachah* in Israel, shalom
—DLR

For Pat, Ray, and Carol
—JW

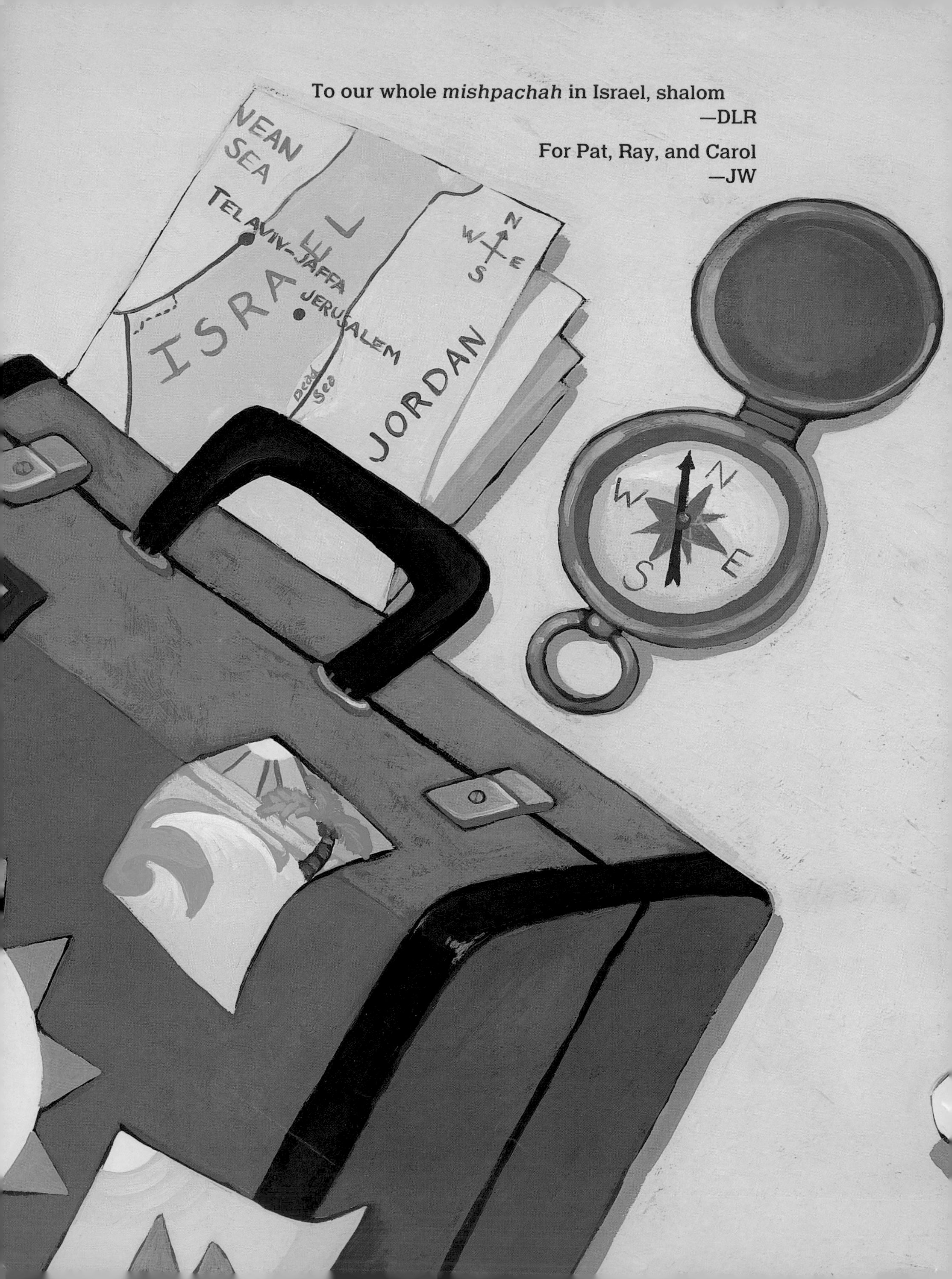

Dinosaur Goes to Israel

Diane Levin Rauchwerger

pictures by Jason Wolff

KAR-BEN
PUBLISHING

I'm leaving for a visit
To *Eretz Yisrael*.
Dino begs to come along.
He's wiggling his tail.

We climb aboard the airplane.
He takes three seats and more.
He must be very comfy.
The whole plane hears him snore.

When we land in Tel Aviv,
Our cousins take us home.

"Todah Rabah," I thank them.
Dino says "*Shalom*."

We drive around the city,
And Dino sees the sand.

He begs to get out at the beach.
His bucket's in his hand.

For lunch we eat falafel,
With salad, chips, and pickles.

I wipe some dribbles off his chin.
He laughs and says it tickles.

Our next stop is Jerusalem.
And Dino is so tall,

He tucks his message way, way up
Atop the Western Wall.

Dino stops to chat with camels,
As we hike around Eilat.
He invites them to go snorkeling,
But they say they'd rather not.

I ride up Mt. Masada.
Dino hikes the snakey path.

We cool off at the Dead Sea.
He enjoys a warm mud bath.

Our last stop is the busy *shuk*
To buy a souvenir.
Dino picks a shofar
To blow on the New Year.

And when we're finally home again,
Dino starts to wail,
"When can we go back again,
To *Eretz Yisrael*?"

KAR-BEN PUBLISHING
A division of Lerner Publishing Group, Inc.
241 First Avenue North
Minneapolis, MN 55401 U.S.A.
800-4KARBEN

Website address: www.karben.com

Library of Congress Cataloging-in-Publication Data

Rauchwerger, Diane Levin.
Dinosaur goes to Israel / by Diane Levin Rauchwerger ; illustrated by Jason Wolff.
p. cm.
Summary: Enthusiastic but accident–prone Dinosaur accompanies a young boy on a visit to Israel.
ISBN 978–0–7613–5133–7 (lib. bdg. : alk. paper)
[1. Stories in rhyme. 2. Israel—Fiction. 3. Dinosaurs—Fiction.] I. Wolff, Jason, ill. II. Title.
PZ8.3.R2323De 2011
[E]—dc22 2009030917

Manufactured in the United States of America
1 – PP – 2/1/13